This book belongs to:

....

....

The Most Muddled Monster

and other stories

Written by
NICOLA BAXTER

Illustrated by
ANDREW WARRINGTON

This is a Parragon Book
This edition published in 2002

Parragon
Queen Street House
4 Queen Street
Bath BA1 1HE, UK

Copyright © Parragon 2000

ISBN 0-75259-501-6

Produced for Parragon by
Nicola Baxter

Designed by Amanda Hawkes
Cover designed by Gemma Hornsby
Cover illustrated by Andrew Everitt- Stewart

Printed in Italy

Contents

The Most Muddled Monster   7

The Missing Monster   33

A Monster Called Mavis   51

A Monster for Me   69

His Majesty the Monster   97

Monster Prints   129

The Most Muddled Monster

Monsters love to win prizes. In fact, it is very hard to say whether it is the winning they love most or the prizes, for monsters are terribly competitive and hate to be beaten at anything. At the end of any monster contest or competition, there is usually a prize-giving ceremony, which all too often becomes a rather ugly occasion. The judges are attacked by the runners-up. The winner is attacked by the losers. Very often the trophy is attacked by those members of the audience who feel they are missing out on a good bit of attacking.

Mrs. Murgle, Headmistress of the Merry Little Monsters Nursery School, was determined to put a stop to the riot that always developed on Sports Day. She was tired of rescuing her staff from hedges and taking cup-winners to casualty to have their cups removed (*usually* from their heads). She longed for the kind of well-run occasion that her sister, who taught baby dragons instead of monsters, frequently boasted about. And the problem, she realized, stemmed from the idea of holding a competition in the first place.

Mrs. Murgle did a lot of reading in the more advanced books about monster children and their development. She soon found that almost everything to do with young monsters was the fault of their parents, a fact she had long suspected. But education, too, had a part to play. Here Mrs. Murgle felt more confident. With careful training, monster children, it seemed, could be made to feel so relaxed and happy that they did not need to bash each other over the head each morning. Mrs. Murgle began to lay her plans.

At the beginning of the summer term at the Merry Little Monsters Nursery School, parents were surprised to receive a long letter from Mrs. Murgle headed "Encourage your little monsters! Make them merry!" There was a lot in the letter about giving praise to little monsters, even when they were being most monsterish.

Mr. Mandrake Monster read the letter over breakfast.

"Phwerrrrrugh!" he said (or words to that effect). "What a load of swiggle! As if any little monster is going to become an angel by being soft on him. That Murgle woman's been out in the sun too long. I always thought she was odd."

"Anything is worth a try," sighed his wife. "You *are* eating your breakfast nicely, Muckworth!"

Muckworth Monster looked up and promptly lost control of his porridge spoon. A large gloop of porridge shot through the air and began to drip very, very slowly off his father's nose. Mr. Mandrake Monster made the kind of noise it is quite impossible to write down and stomped off to work.

That morning, in Mrs. Murgle's class, the new regime did seem to be having some effect. When three little monsters began to bite the table legs, Mrs. Murgle praised them for not biting the chairs. The three monsters looked at her in disgust and went off to do some painting. There was no interest in a table leg that they were *allowed* to bite. Margarina Monster, who was licking the windowpanes, was patted on the head.

"I'll get you a cloth, so you can clean them properly," said Mrs. Murgle. Margarina sat down quietly with a book instead.

Of course, none of this lasted more than a second or two, but it was enough for Mrs. Murgle to feel she really should persevere. She was surer than ever that support from parents was essential. Another letter went home with the little monsters at the end of the week. It was headed, "Praise, praise and praise again! Then praise some more!" Mr. Mandrake Monster stuffed his into the toes of some too-big boots.

Meanwhile, Mrs. Murgle was reading more about the tender characters of her pupils. It seemed that it was important for every little monster to do really well at *something*. Next morning, she gave Mully, a little monster who loved to paint pictures of rubbish bins, a special prize for artistic effort. There was uproar at once. Every monster in the building headed for the paint pots. In the fight that happened when they got there, most of the school was redecorated in a range of interesting shades. Mrs. Murgle hid under the desk and decided that her approach needed to be more subtle.

It was in the middle of the following night that Mrs. Murgle had her Great Idea. She lost no time in sending out another letter to parents. This time the heading read, "Your children are the mostest! Make the most of them!" Mr. Mandrake Monster looked at it with horror.

"The woman has lost all grasp of grammar," he said. "She's not fit to teach little monsters, merry or otherwise. And in our case," he went on, looking up at Muckworth, "quite definitely otherwise."

Muckworth was morosely staring at his feet, wondering why his shoes looked wrong. He'd tried putting them on the opposite feet, in case that was the problem, but it hadn't occurred to him that they were on backwards.

When her husband had gone to work and Muckworth had been delivered to Mrs. Murgle, Mrs. Monster smoothed out the letter and looked at it in more detail. Rather to her surprise, much of it made some sort of sense.

"Little monsters," she read, "need to feel pride in what they do. If they are shouted at or ignored, they will not grow up to be fine monsters of the future. That is why I am beginning the 'mostest' scheme. I am convinced that every precious little monster has a feature of his or her character that can be praised without reservation. As soon as you say to your little monster, 'You are the most talented/ beautiful/extraordinary/hilarious/what-ever-seems-appropriate little monster in the world!' he or she will begin to blossom. Mrs. Monster thought about it. She would dearly love to see Muckworth blossom,

but she was very doubtful that this could make it happen. Still, if there was even the chance of a light dusting of blossom, she must try it. Now, what was Muckworth the mostest at?

Mrs. Marigold Monster was still thinking when she went to collect her son at twelve o'clock. She was still thinking when Mr. Mandrake Monster came home at six o'clock. She was still thinking when Mr. Mandrake Monster's snores were rattling the window panes. What on earth was Muckworth the mostest at?

 Finally, Marigold could stand it no longer. She woke her husband (never a very good idea) and put the problem before him.

"I can't believe you woke me up to ask me this!" he squawked. "Anyway, it's obvious. He's the most stupid child I've ever met."

"Oh no, dear," said Marigold at once. "Surely you'd have to say that Mrs. Mudmop's youngest is more stupid than Muckworth."

"That is true," admitted Mr. Monster slowly. "Well, he's the daftest monster I know ... except for Uncle Mudge, of course, and my brother's father-in-law."

"Anyway," remarked his wife. "You couldn't really say that Muckworth was stupid or daft. He just finds it difficult to sort things out. I really think it's because there is too much going on in his head, not too little."

Mr. Monster made one of those noises again and went back to sleep. Next morning at breakfast, however, he suddenly lowered his paper and said, "Slovenly?"

"My cousin Maudle," replied his wife, shaking her head.

"Slothful?"

"Miffle Merton at the garage."

"True. Awkward?"

"My dear, you yourself…."

"All right. All right." Mr. Monster got up and went to work.

Muckworth, who had no idea what they were talking about, tried to work out which foot went first when he was walking.

At the Nursery School, Mrs. Murgle was finding her fine new scheme was not without problems. The monsters were all shown how to make their own rosettes. So far, so good. When Mrs. Murgle had decided what they were the mostest at, she wrote it in big letters in the middle of the rosettes. So far, not so bad. After that, the little monsters were allowed to wear their rosettes. So far, so disastrous.

Those little monsters who didn't yet have rosettes were resentful of those who did. There were tussles. There was name-calling. There was a floor littered with scraps of what had been rosettes. There was a tired and emotional Mrs. Murgle, seeing her famous plan collapsing around her. No one was very happy.

Once again, Mrs. Murgle went home to think about things. That night, she once again had an inspiration. The whole problem was that all little monsters must be made to feel cherished at the same time. Or at least, on the same occasion. Otherwise, those who had not succeeded quite naturally felt aggrieved. What was needed was a rosette-giving ceremony, a chance for parents and children alike to feel a sense of pride and achievement. In short, a prize-giving. Yes, Mrs. Murgle had a very short memory!

She had forgotten, as you, I am sure, have not, that it was precisely because prize-givings were such a disaster that she had thought of her "mostest" plan in the first place. Perhaps Mr. Mandrake Monster was right about Mrs. Murgle.

The next day, parents once more received a letter from the Merry Little Monsters Nursery School.

"I'll soon have enough of these to paper the living room," muttered young Muckworth's father. "What is she saying this time?"

The letter was headed, "A chance to shine! Support your children in their first steps to SUCCESS!"

"It's a very bad sign when someone breaks into capital letters," commented Mr. Mandrake Monster. "I told you, that woman is unhinged. What, after all, is Muckworth going to win his rosette for?"

As a matter of fact, that question had been troubling Mrs. Murgle ever since she began making her prize-winning lists. She had a whole pile of rosettes for the Most Inventive, Most Charming, Most Amusing and Most Original little monsters. Of course, "most amusing" was a matter of personal taste, and not everyone would find a shoe full of marmalade funny, but Mrs. Murgle was prepared to be generous in pursuit of her ideals.

Muckworth Monster was the very last one on Mrs. Murgle's long list. Like his parents, she found it very, very hard to think of anything that he was the mostest at. In desperation, with only one day to go before the prize-giving, Mrs. Murgle began to follow Muckworth around.

As Mrs. Murgle lurked, Muckworth looked down to where a little snail was slithering slowly across the playground. Most Patient Little Monster?

"They *do* move slowly, don't they?" said Mrs. Murgle encouragingly.

"What do?" asked Muckworth, who had in fact been wondering how stones got into Tarmac. He wandered off.

Mrs. Murgle watched Muckworth at drink-and-monster-munchies time. Most Appealing Table Manners? Definitely not. Most Disgusting Table Manners? Well, no, there were several little monsters higher in the league for *that*.

At going-home time, Mrs. Murgle watched hopefully as Muckworth put his coat on. Most Competent Dresser? No. She hovered as he greeted his mother. Most Affectionate Little Monster? No again. In fact, Muckworth seemed a little vague about which one his mother was. The anxious teacher watched as her young pupil set off down the road with Mrs. Marigold Monster. Most Careful Road

Crossing? Aaagh, no! Mrs. Murgle had to close her eyes as Muckworth dithered alarmingly in front of an approaching truck. As the mother and son disappeared around the corner, Mrs. Murgle had to admit defeat. She comforted herself that of all the little monsters in her care, this one was so vague and confused, he would probably not notice if he did not receive a prize. It wasn't strictly in line with her ideas, but sometimes one simply had to be a little flexible.

On the day of the prize-giving, Mrs. Murgle was at her most efficient. Parents and little monsters were ushered into their seats. Latecomers were hurried along. Whisperers were shushed. Mrs. Murgle stood on the platform with her pile of rosettes and greeted the expectant crowd. She was a little disconcerted to find that Mr. Mandrake Monster and his wife were sitting in the front row. And the only word to describe Mr. Mandrake Monster's expression was "glowering". With some misgivings, Mrs. Murgle began to call the little monsters to the stage to receive their "mostest" rosettes.

Two little monsters from the end, Mr. Mandrake Monster's expression had moved from glowering to thunderous. Mrs. Murgle led the applause for the Most Energetic Little Monster as he bounced off the stage.

"And now," said Mrs. Murgle, her voice quavering as she prayed for last-minute inspiration, "we have our very last prize, for our dear Muckworth Monster. Come along, Muckworth, up here, dear!"

Muckworth rose from his seat and meandered towards the stage. At the steps, he hesitated, thought of something he really must tell his mother and set off back to his seat.

"No, no, dear, this way!" called Mrs. Murgle. Muckworth only heard the last word, but he heard it as "sway". Rocking from side to side, he wafted back towards the stage again.

"What are you *doing*?" cried Mrs. Murgle. And just when she had given up all hope, an idea suddenly popped into her head. "Come on," she cried, "here is your prize for being the Most Muddled Little Monster!"

As Muckworth accepted his prize, Mr. Mandrake Monster leapt to his feet. "No one calls a son of mine muddled!" he bellowed, which was most unfair, when you consider the terms that he himself had suggested to describe young Muckworth.

Mrs Murgle tried to stay calm. Well, perhaps it hadn't been the most tactful thing to say. But one look at the rest of the audience, and she could see that things were turning ugly. The monster mothers and fathers watching had been vaguely aware that something was missing from the proceedings. Now they knew what it was … pushing, shoving, calling monsters names, tripping monsters up, in short, doing all the things that were traditional at prize-giving ceremonies, and doing them with enthusiasm. Within seconds, the lack was no more. The noise was terrible. The furniture was shredded. The smiles on the faces of the parent monsters were horrible to see. All the monsters except Mrs. Murgle were having a very good time indeed.

Several hours later, when all the monster families had gone home to apply bandages and discuss the most memorable parts of the event, Mrs. Murgle sat among the wreckage and sobbed. Somehow, in spite of her good intentions, things were much worse now than when she tried to make them better. She had failed as a teacher and as a monster. It was dreadful.

All at once, Mrs. Murgle became aware that she was not alone. Someone was sitting in the corner of the room and, yes, singing! It was Muckworth, and he was beaming all over his face.

"Why are you still here?" asked Mrs. Murgle.

"Because I like school," explained Muckworth. "I like school and I like all the things we do here and most of all I like being the mostest at something. Only since I've been the mostest I don't feel muddled somehow. So maybe I'm not the mostest. But it doesn't matter."

Mrs. Murgle was amazed. After all, Muckworth was only four and what he was saying almost made sense. The teacher beamed as she realized that her theories had not been completely wrong after all.

"I like school, too, Muckworth," she said. "Let me take you home. Best foot forward!"

And it just shows how much better Muckworth felt that he knew straight away which his best foot was…

The
Missing
Monster

One day Joshua Robert Koval found a monster. At least, he said he did. He put it in his pocket to bring it to school and on the way he lost it. That's the story he told us. Of course, not one of us believed him. I mean, how many monsters have *you* found recently?

"You're such a liar, J.R.," said Martha, who believed in speaking her mind. "No one ever believes what you say. Remember you told us your dad was an airline pilot and then we found out he was a boring old accountant?"

"Well…" said Joshua.

"Well…" said Annalise, whose father was also an accountant but not, to her mind, boring. Not *very* boring, at least.

But Martha was steaming on.

"Remember you said you had a bike for your birthday with dozens of gears and racing wheels? I wonder why we've never actually seen it!"

"Well…" said Joshua. But Martha was going on.

"Remember when you told us your mum was a brilliant pianist and would play at the school concert and then she had flu and couldn't come? *Very* convenient!"

"Well…" said Joshua. But Martha was leading us all back into school, not giving Josh a chance to reply. To be fair to him, he kept it up right to the very end—

pretending about the monster, I mean. As we crashed through the swing doors, I could hear him wailing.

"Won't anyone help me look for my monster?" It made me laugh.

At the end of the afternoon, we all strolled home together as usual. Martha lives nearest to the school, so she wasn't with us any more when we went around the corner of Fisher Street and saw Joshua crawling on his hands and knees on the dusty pavement.

"I didn't know he wore contacts," said Annalise, who did and liked everyone to know it.

"Neither did I," said Harry. "But remember he's been picked for the team on Saturday. We'd better help him find them."

"He's probably only lost one," said Annalise, with the airy tone of someone who knows all about losing contact lenses.

We all slowed down as we got near to J.R., not wanting to tread on something that might be worth a goal or two at the weekend.

"How can we help?" I asked, trying to ignore a snort from Annalise that meant "Some of us *know* how to help."

"I think it was just here I lost it," said J.R. "I think we should creep forward very carefully and try not to make any noise. It might not like noise. You never know. Especially with its little tiny ears."

For a moment we all thought he had lost his mind. Since when did contact lenses have ears? Then, all together, we realized he really had lost his mind. He was talking about the monster!

Annalise scrambled up in disgust and stamped her foot.

"Well, I hope I've squashed it!" she shouted, which was a bit illogical when you consider that she didn't believe it was there in the first place.

"You can't have," replied J.R. "It's very fast on its feet and it'll be miles away by now, with you making all that noise."

The others made various noises of their own to show that they thought the whole thing was ridiculous and ran off down the street, shouting things about J.R.'s state of mind that were very far from complimentary.

I don't know why I stayed. I guess it was something to do with the really sad look on his face. And the fact that even now his eyes were darting right and left in case he spotted something. If he was acting, he was Oscar standard. In the back of my mind, I was wondering if I should take

him to a doctor or something. As I tried to work out how to do it, J.R. spoke again.

"You see," he said, "I've never found one before."

"No, neither have I," I said. I mean, I thought I should sort of humour him, and anyway, it was true.

"I thought I might be a bit more popular if I had a monster."

This was getting embarrassing. "You are popular, Josh," I said, crossing my fingers. "It's just the things you say, you know, like Martha was saying this morning. It sounds like you're trying to pretend you're better than us and then, when it turns out it's not even true, kids aren't happy. You can understand it."

"But it is true," said J.R.

"Oh, right." Sometimes you just can't help people. I decided to drop the subject and turned to go home.

"It was orange with three eyes. One of them was sort of sticking out of the top of its head. And it had purple bits as well, but I wasn't sure what they were."

He was so convincing that before I could stop myself I had asked, "How big was it?"

"About as big as my thumb," he replied. "But it hopped about a lot so it was hard to see everything. And anyway, I was kind of surprised."

"You would be," I muttered.

Things were worse than I thought. It did seem to me that a doctor was a good idea. The guy didn't have many friends at the moment. He wouldn't have any at all if this went on. And anyway, I could see he was on a slippery slope. You start with little lies about your mum and dad and a birthday present. Then you start seeing monsters. Who knows what happens next? Frankly, I didn't want to be around to find out.

Joshua lived on the other side of town, but I didn't think it was safe to leave him on his own. I just mooched along beside him, pretending it was the kind of thing I did every day.

My plan was to arrive home with him, wander in when he did, and try to have a quiet word with his mum or dad. It wasn't a no-risk plan. In my experience, parents often don't want to hear

bad news about their children, especially
as bad as this. I remember being voted the
one to tell Mrs. Evans about Harry
crunching his bike into her rose bed, and
she acted like it was *my* fault!

Josh and I walked slowly towards
his house. Most of the way, he was talking.
It didn't make a lot of sense to me so I
tried not to listen. For all I knew he was
seeing monsters all over the place.

It turned out that Josh lived in a
pretty nice house. There were steps up to
the front door and two big urn things with
flowers in them on either side. There was
also a *really* nice bike chained to the fence.

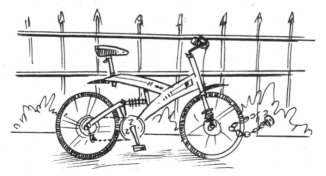

I slowed down to look at it. Josh turned around with a sigh.

"Dad won't let me bring it to school," he said. "He says it will get nicked."

"He's right," I said, beginning to feel the ground was shifting under my feet. "I guess you have to be a bit cautious if you're an accountant. Bikes are money, after all."

"Not Bill, *Dad*," said Joshua. "Bill's the accountant. He's married to my mum. He's okay and everything, but he's not Dad. I don't get to see Dad much, because he's always flying off somewhere, but he brings me brilliant presents when he comes back."

My mind had started whirling unpleasantly. It wasn't much helped by the incredibly loud noise that hit my ears as soon as Josh opened the front door.

"That's Mum," said Josh.

"Wow! If I played my stereo that loud, Dad would take it away for *weeks*!" I shouted above the din.

"It's not a stereo," whispered J.R. (Whispering worked better than shouting somehow. You wouldn't think it would, but it did.) "Look!"

He threw open a door on the right and the noise hurtled out to meet us. Inside, a smallish woman was playing the

piano in what I can only call a very *positive* way. I'd never heard anything like it.

My ears were still jangling when she suddenly crashed to a stop. She grinned at the sight of my face.

"Sorry," she said. "Concert halls are huge, you see. You have to really *play*."

I tell you, that woman certainly *played*. By now, my ideas about Josh had got a bit messed up. I was feeling shock and, yes, a bit guilty for all the things I'd thought about him in the past. Then I remembered the monster. No, hang on, this guy was definitely a trombone short of a brass band. I still needed to have a word with his mum. As I thought about this, I realized she was talking to me.

"It's nice to meet one of Josh's friends at last. Come into the kitchen and have something to eat."

She seemed really nice. I followed her down a big hallway.

"I'll just dash upstairs," said Josh. "I told it where I live, so you never know, it might just have come back here. Don't say anything, will you?"

Well, that made things difficult for a second, but luckily he shot off before I had a chance to reply, so maybe I hadn't really *promised*.

I started to think of ways of broaching the subject with Mrs Koval. I wanted to lead up to it gradually, but Josh could be back at any moment.

"Sit down," said the poor woman. "I was just going to make a sandwich."

I sat down at a huge pine table. In the middle was a big wooden bowl full of fruit. Somehow, I couldn't look her in the face as I told her the news, so I kept my eyes fixed on an apple and two tangerines.

"Actually, Mrs. Koval, I was hoping for the chance to talk to you," I began.

It was at this point that one of the tangerines suddenly sat up. It had three eyes and some purple bits.

You won't be surprised to know that by this time I was clutching the table so hard I left nail marks on it.

"Yes?" You could tell Mrs. Koval was puzzled.

"I... I..." was all I could get out, when Joshua came into the room. He sat down on the other side of the table and cheerfully accepted his mother's offer of a cheese sandwich.

Meanwhile, I was making wild eye movements to J.R. to tell him about what I had just seen. Mrs. Koval looked at me curiously, then turned back to finish her sandwich-making. At once, I pointed to the fruit bowl and mouthed to J.R.

"THE MONSTER!"

To do him justice, he didn't cry out or leap up or anything. He leaned over for a good look and gave me a big grin and a thumbs-up sign. With a sinking heart, I realized that if he was unhinged, so was I. Both of us were seeing an orange monster with three eyes and purple bits. I looked at it again. At least, I tried to. The monster had gone, and it wasn't just pretending to be a tangerine.

Under Mrs. Koval's astonished gaze, we made a thorough search of the kitchen. We searched the house, the garden and the entire street. That was three weeks ago. These days, Josh and I are best friends and the rest of the gang won't speak to us. But then, we hardly mind. We're on a mission to find a monster and we intend to carry on until we do.

You think that's really sad? Just be careful. Who knows what you might see tomorrow!

A Monster Called Mavis

DANCING ACADEMY

Turn your ugly ducklings into swans!

Mavis was a monster with ambitions. She wanted to be astonishingly beautiful. She wanted to be a star. But more than anything else, she wanted to be human. You will have to take a good look at Mavis to understand why none of these ambitions was ever likely to succeed. You may need to prepare yourself:

Feel free at this point to break off for a glass of water or a quiet lie down. No? Okay, here is what happened to Mavis.

Now, there *are* beautiful monsters, certainly, but they only look beautiful to other monsters. Mavis was *not* beautiful to monsters or anyone else. Even her mother, who loved her dearly, would not have said she was attractive.

"It isn't looks that count, darling," she would say. "It's personality. Anyway, you don't have to be beautiful to be a star. Look at Agula Flanthrop."

Agula Flanthrop was indeed a very big star in the monster movie world. It is true that she specialized in playing various different kinds of slimy sluglike creatures (and not much acting was involved), but even so, her face was well known. But Mavis didn't want to play sluglike creatures. She wanted to be the kind of star who lay on couches and was fed grapes by servants so dazzled by her beauty they didn't need to be paid.

Mavis read all the movie magazines avidly, and whenever she heard about a new beauty treatment that one of the stars had used to great success, she wanted to try it for herself. As Mavis did not have movie-star money, she sometimes had to improvise. When Plak Malong (star of a monster medical series) raved about the advantages of a mango face mask, Mavis copied her—but used carrots instead. The result—an unappealing orange colour replacing Mavis's usual green tones—was not encouraging. Mavis drew the line at trying to do her own facelift (despite the fact that Mlaglug Clog looked marvellous at seventy after five of them) but she did experiment with tying her ears up over her head with string. It certainly did wonders for her chin, but the anguish on the rest of her face hardly made it worthwhile.

Then, when browsing one day on the Monsternet, Mavis came across an advertisement for a ballet school. The main picture showed three little girls in pink tutus looking delightful. The caption got straight to the point: "Let us turn your ugly ducklings into sylphlike swans!" it trilled. "Success guaranteed. An education in grace and deportment for every girl."

Mavis only understood half what she read, but the magic words "success guaranteed" seemed to spring off the screen. Before she had consulted her mother or had any time to think sensibly, Mavis had pressed the button and booked herself into the school.

There was only one problem. No, that's not true. There were hundreds of problems and Mavis's ears were only two of them, but the main problem was that the school was for humans. Mavis wasn't, by any stretch of the imagination, human. But as being human was what Mavis wanted more than anything else, she assumed that the school would handle that little difficulty as well. Success, after all, was guaranteed.

When a big parcel arrived for Mavis containing her school uniform, she could hardly contain her excitement. There were white wafty garments. There were frothy pink tutus. There were dainty dancing slippers (roughly a third of the size of Mavis's great feet) and frilly ribbons for tying up her hair (not, with short green tufts, entirely useful). Last but not least, there was a dramatic blue velvet cloak to go over everything else. Mavis clambered into a wafty white number, gave up with the slippers, and swathed herself in her cloak for her first day.

As she lined up with the other girls, she towered head and shoulders above them, but she did her best to remember everything she had ever read about poise and posture. Holding her head high, Mavis pranced into the school, her feet and everything else scarcely hidden by the hooded cloak.

Mavis enjoyed her first term. The other girls avoided her, it is true, but that was probably because of her smell. I'm afraid personal hygiene isn't an idea that monsters take to. The teacher was a very elderly lady, with short sight and an even shorter memory. Several times she asked Mavis why she was dancing in flippers, but as she was also very hard of hearing, she never heard Mavis's wounded replies.

As the weeks passed, Mavis felt very confident that she was gaining in grace. She was less sure about deportment, which sounded like something to do with a shop, but she put her heart and soul into her dancing. Several of the other girls were injured in the process, but that, of course, didn't worry Mavis.

In fact, very little worried Mavis. She wasn't unduly concerned when the floor collapsed one day under the strain of her pirouettes. She had drilled herself through a vital support and was lucky not to bring the building tumbling down about her ears.

She wasn't very upset when the other girls got together a legal petition to have her removed from the school, although she was glad when it was turned down on a technicality.

She wasn't offended when the lady who taught Make-up for the Stage assumed she had arrived with an effective "sea monster" make-up already in place. No, Mavis was perfectly happy rampaging

down the long corridors and crushing all
the toes that got in her way.

Mavis's attempts to be human were,
if anything, even less successful than her
dancing. The other girls seemed to do a lot
of giggling. Mavis tried but made a sound
somewhere between a cow stuck in a ditch
and a foghorn. Her ancient teacher asked
if she was unwell.

The girls seemed
completely obsessed by
clothes as well. Once
again, Mavis was at a bit
of a disadvantage. After
one brief session in town,
looking for something
pretty to wear, she decided
that there was a lot to be
said for mail order. Having
sales assistants running
screaming from you in

the changing rooms isn't encouraging for a shopper, especially one who is a little self-conscious about her size and figure. And anyway, nothing seemed to fit.

Unfortunately, although mail order solved the first problem, it did nothing for the second one. In the end, Mavis bought several pairs of coloured sheets and twisted them together in original ways to create new costumes. After there was an outbreak of mass hysteria one evening (Mavis was spotted wandering down a corridor late one night and taken for a ghost, an ogre or a vampire by every girl who saw her), Mavis gave up on *haute couture* and went back to wearing her school cloak at all times. Monsters are not renowned for their table manners, so it did become fairly gruesome after a while, but the ancient teacher summed it up when she said, "Well, it suits *you*, dear!"

In the second half of the term, all lessons were focussed on the end-of-term performance. Mavis, much to her surprise, was given an important role in the third act. (She never fully grasped that she was in fact supposed to be representing a flamingo, and as the tallest in the class was the obvious choice. The other girls were being doves.)

Mavis practised and practised. Her *pas de chat* was anything but catlike. Her *grand jeté* anything but grand (and it wasn't very big either), but Mavis felt that she

was dancing superbly and, as her teacher often told her, confidence is *so* important.

The evening of the first performance arrived at last. The hall was filled with the expectant buzz of two hundred proud mothers. The girls all giggled anxiously as they got ready.

Mavis struggled into her pink tutu and did her warm-up exercises, almost demolishing the scenery in the process. Then the stage manager called for silence, the orchestra struck up, and the performance began.

Backstage, Mavis bit her nails and then her toenails. All too soon, the music that heralded her arrival on the stage began. Mavis galumphed into the wings and got ready to make her grand entrance.

As she thundered on to the stage, Mavis heard the gasps of two hundred mothers with excellent eyesight. As she twirled in front of them, she heard them gasp again. Could this … could this … was this some kind of joke?

The chattering of the audience soon became so loud that the orchestra stopped playing. Mavis stood on tiptoes and waited for the music to start again. But it didn't. The flummoxed flamingo looked at the audience. The audience looked back, hardly able to believe its four hundred eyes. What on earth was going on?

"Curtain! Curtain!" hissed the School Principal, furiously gesturing at the stage manager. Unfortunately, Mavis heard and saw her too. In an effort to be helpful, and dimly aware that all was not as it should be, she rushed forward to draw the big velvet curtains.

The curtains were big and heavy. But so was Mavis. In her eagerness, first one and then the other came whooshing down. If they had fallen on top of the unlucky monster, all might yet have been well, for the audience still believed it was having a huge and horrible dream.

No, the curtains fell outwards. The orchestra, the conductor and the School Principal were completely covered. The sound of crashing cymbals and a muffled thud that might just have been someone falling into the bottom of a bass drum were all that could be heard. Then there was a dreadful silence.

Mavis sighed and scratched her hairy armpits. Several mothers in the front row fainted. It wasn't, Mavis thought, quite as easy to pretend to be human as she had imagined. Hoping to get the audience back on her side, she smiled broadly.

It was a dreadful mistake. At the sight of three rows of monster teeth leering at them across the footlights, the entire school audience headed for the exits. There was quite a lot of screaming as well. Sadly, Mavis tucked up her tutu and set off for home. She had wanted to cause a stir, but this wasn't quite what she had intended.

"I think I'd be better in films," said Mavis. "Hollywood, here I come!"

A Monster for Me

Aunts can be surprising, and Elspeth Mary Miller's Aunt Madge was more surprising than most. Elspeth Mary was a girl who liked to be unusual. When all her friends at school were wearing pink and lemon, Elspeth bought a black dress and sewed purple patches all over it. When they bought little strappy sandals with sparkly bits on the heels, Elspeth found a pair of her granny's old army boots and painted one black and one white. Her father had long ago given up trying to make her do ordinary things, and to tell the truth, he quite liked having a truly extraordinary daughter.

But when she met Aunt Madge, Elspeth realized that she had only just scratched the surface of being unusual. Elspeth's father described Aunt Madge as "eccentric", but that was only because she was Elspeth's mother's sister and he was being kind. "Several sandwiches short of a picnic" was how he described her to his friends. Even so, it was hard not to like Madge, especially as she looked so much like her sister Susan, who had died when Elspeth was only a baby.

Aunt Madge didn't drive a car like ordinary people. She drove a secondhand hearse, which she had painted yellow. She said it had lots of room in the back, but Elspeth's father told her it was macabre, and when Elspeth had looked it up in her dictionary, she had to agree with him.

Another odd thing about Aunt Madge was that she always wore the same clothes—a navy blue skirt and a navy blue top, and a navy blue coat when it was cold. For a long time, Elspeth thought that they really were the same clothes, and that her aunt never washed them or mended them or put them away for the winter. But after she visited Aunt Madge's flat, she realized that there were cupboards and cupboards full of navy blue clothes, all exactly the same. "I buy them a dozen at a time," said her aunt. "It saves time."

Aunt Madge was pretty odd when it came to food, too. She only ate yellow things. She said it was like eating sunshine.

She loved bananas, lemons and sweetcorn. But she wouldn't touch a strawberry or a piece of chocolate cake. Feeding her had been very difficult the first time she came to stay, but Elspeth's father was a resourceful man and soon found that yellow food colouring thrown into potatoes, rice or pasta solved the problem nicely. "No need to tell your aunt, though," he warned his daughter as he discreetly disposed of the empty bottles.

The most exciting thing about Aunt Madge was what she did for a living.

She was a composer, and quite a famous one. Elspeth was very proud indeed when a short piece called *Elspeth Mary Miller's*

Three Minute Mazurka was played at the opening of the new City Hall. It did seem a little strange that most of the piece seemed to be performed on old kettles with teaspoons, but the critics loved it.

When Elspeth Mary had her eighth birthday, she came across her father and Aunt Madge arguing in the kitchen. At least, Aunt Madge was arguing and her father was repeating himself, which was something Elspeth had very often noticed when she had a case to put to him.

"The girl is old enough, now, Patrick," said Aunt Madge firmly.

"No," said Mr. Miller.

"She is responsible and sensible," said Aunt Madge.

"No," said Mr. Miller.

"I would make sure she looked after it properly," said Aunt Madge.

"No," said Mr. Miller.

"And you wouldn't have to worry about a thing."

"No."

"I had one at very much her age."

"No."

"How can you be so stubborn? Have you thought what Susan would have wanted?"

"No!"

"What on earth are you talking about?" asked Elspeth, hoisting herself up to sit on the table with her legs swinging.

"Nothing," said her father.

"I was saying that you were old enough now to have a pet," said Aunt Madge. "It would be nice for you to have something of your own to look after."

"Yes!" cried Elspeth. "Oh, yes!"

Mr. Miller threw the teacloth over his head in despair.

"Madge, you are a most provoking woman. I've said No, and that's the end of it. All right?"

But in his heart, he knew that the battle was lost. He could hold out against Madge. He could hold out against Elspeth. But the two of them together were a truly formidable team. Mentally, he prepared himself to go out and buy a hamster cage.

But Elspeth, as usual, wanted to be different. "I don't want a kitten or a puppy or a hamster or a rabbit like other kids," she told her aunt. "I'd like something a bit

more out of the ordinary. I'm going to look into reptiles."

Mr. Miller groaned and left the room. Already he had visions of pythons in the pantry and lizards running up his trouser legs. Suddenly an ordinary kitten seemed very appealing indeed. On second thoughts, he retraced his steps and opened the door.

"Elspeth," he said, "I want to make it perfectly clear here and now that I am not having a walrus in the house."

Then he shut the door and went off to his workshop.

Elspeth and her aunt exchanged a knowing glance.

"A walrus isn't a reptile," said Elspeth, wrinkling her nose.

"Just between you and me, darling," replied Aunt Madge, "I sometimes think your father is becoming slightly eccentric. He's not like other people at all."

Elspeth couldn't think of a sensible reply to this in the circumstances, so she went back to thinking about pets as her aunt finished putting the dishes away. But the more she thought about it, the more difficult it got. There simply didn't seem to be enough pets to choose from.

"You see," she told her aunt, "other people have things like snakes and lizards. They even have spiders and tarantulas. I'd like something that other people *don't* have. Only I think there are rules against keeping polar bears."

"Polar bears aren't reptiles either," said Aunt Madge.

"No, I know that, it was just an example," Elspeth replied crossly. "I know! I could have a chameleon. It would change colour to match my dress."

"Well, that's true." Aunt Madge looked thoughtful. "But wouldn't that mean that no one could see it?"

Elspeth nodded grimly. "The trouble is," she said, "that if you're not allowed to keep a really rare animal, then any animal you have is bound to be common."

Aunt Madge had to confess that this was true.

"What surprises me, Elspeth," she said, "knowing how much you like to be different, is that you are thinking of an *animal* as a pet at all. That's what's usual, surely?"

Elspeth regarded her aunt with some concern. There was eccentricity and there was being completely off the wall. Was she seriously suggesting that Elspeth went around with a rock or a piece of cheese on a lead? Pets *were* animals, weren't they? She imagined herself saying to friends, "Have you seen my pet radish/mattress/lamp-post?" Even she couldn't get away with that.

"I can't have a pet radish," she told her aunt coldly, sounding very much like her father.

Now it was Aunt Madge's turn to look puzzled. "Why on earth would you want that?" she asked. "No, I was thinking of monsters."

"Monsters?"

"Yes, monsters. Wouldn't a pet monster be different?"

"It *would* be different," said Elspeth slowly, in the tone you would talk to a small child, "but it wouldn't be *possible*, would it? I mean, monsters don't exist."

"Haven't you heard my *March of the Monsters*?" asked Aunt Madge in pained tones. "Do you think I made it up entirely, without inspiration from the real thing? Surely not!"

"You mean the piece that sounds like a lot of cutlery being dropped?" asked Elspeth. "I never did understand why it was called *March of the Monsters*. What do you mean, 'the real thing'?"

"I will pass over that reference to my masterpiece," replied Aunt Madge with a certain crispness. "I can see that your education, dear child, has been badly neglected. If your dear mother had been alive today, she would have taught you all about monsters. She had one herself as a

child, although I never liked it. It had a terrible fondness for munching piano keys. Dreadfully annoying. You do have to be careful when choosing a monster. And that is why you need the guidance of an expert."

"Who?" asked Elspeth, thoroughly bewildered now.

"Me!" cried Aunt Madge. "Come on! We'll have to hurry to catch them. Most monsters are in bed by half-past five.

It's something to do with their monster metabolism. Quick!"

Elspeth hurtled after her aunt and into the big yellow van. She preferred to think of it that way.

"There are lots of places you can spot monsters," said her driver, swerving dangerously across the road, "but rubbish dumps are the best. It's astonishing how many people throw them out, thinking they're a bit of old carpet or something. But then, if they will sleep half the time, I suppose…"

Gripping the door handle hard, poor Elspeth tried hard to get a grip on reality as well. Somewhere between coming into the kitchen half an hour ago and dashing off on this nightmare drive, something had gone seriously wrong. She shut her eyes and tried to stay calm. How she wished she had done those first aid classes. There might have been something on restraining people who had totally flipped.

The rubbish dump was almost deserted when the yellow hearse drew up. The setting sun was casting a red glow over the heaps of miscellaneous junk and smelly plastic bags. Elspeth shuddered, but Aunt Madge was glowing with an alarming enthusiasm.

"Open the doors, child," she said. "I can play it on the tape machine in the hearse and turn the volume up."

"Play what?"

But Aunt Madge was pushing a tape of *March of the Monsters* into the machine and twiddling the knobs. Suddenly a noise like a crate of cymbals being dropped from a great height filled the car—and the whole area.

"They'll recognize it, you see," said Aunt Madge. "I'm very well known in monster circles. This is a very popular piece at monster weddings."

Elspeth pulled her coat up over her ears and tried to think of ways of escaping. She was miles from home. Did Aunt Madge have a mobile phone? It seemed unlikely somehow.

Elspeth was just on the point of screaming, feeling that even the help of one of the dodgy-looking characters still wandering around the dump was better than being trapped in a car with a woman who had lost her mind, when something quite extraordinary happened.

A small monster jumped on to the bonnet and waved.

Elspeth blinked.

Another monster, slightly larger than the first and with four sets of arms, joined the first and giggled shyly.

As the final clashing chords of *March of the Monsters* died away, a third monster, with six red legs and a trunk, clambered up beside the other two. As far as it was possible to tell with a creature whose mouth looked very like an eye, he was grinning.

"There," said Aunt Madge, "what did I tell you? Have you got anything to give them?"

Elspeth recovered her voice with difficulty.

"What sort of thing?"

"I don't know, the kind of thing that monsters like. Old chewing gum. A comb. Bus tickets. Anything."

Elspeth hunted in her pockets and came up with a hairslide in the shape of a

bat and three mints that had got gummed together and covered in fluff.

"That will be fine," said her aunt. And the monsters shuffled forward to receive their presents.

"Thanks very much," said the first monster in perfect English. "My name's Mrrmg. What's yours?"

Elspeth told him, wondering whether it was possible for madness to be catching and, if so, was there an antidote?

"That name is terribly difficult to pronounce," said Mrrmg. "Forgive me if I get it wrong, my dear. Now, how can we help you?"

Aunt Madge exchanged a few more pleasantries before getting down to the matter in hand.

"This child," she said, "who is, on the whole, not a bad child, and shows some signs of sense, as you can see by her odd shoes, is looking for a monster to come and live with her. I promise you that she'll be kind, and I, of course, will visit regularly to make sure that everything is as it should be."

The monsters nodded and looked pleased. They whispered and hooted among themselves.

"There is a young monster," said the spokesmonster, "who has sadly recently lost his mother. An unfortunate incident with a carpet beater. He would dearly love a new home, although I would have to ask about your cleaning arrangements. Not surprisingly, he's very wary of vacuum cleaners and the like now."

"I can assure you," said Aunt Madge, "that cleaning in this household is minimal. Once or twice a year at the most."

Elspeth opened her mouth to protest, but she had to admit it was true. Neither she nor her father were very keen on clearing up or cleaning down.

Just at that moment, a fourth monster, smaller than the rest, jumped on to the car with a little squeak.

"Ah," said the chief monster. "This is the young chap I was talking about. His name is Brrrggch."

Elspeth smiled. The little monster was adorable. He had two twinkly eyes, two smiley mouths, and a blue furry body, although his hands and feet were yellow. He looked shy but he smiled back.

Half an hour later, Elspeth found herself driving home with the monster carefully strapped in beside her. She knew what he liked to eat (orange peel and tooth-paste) and where he liked to sleep (in an old slipper, the smellier the better). She felt very, very happy to have him beside her. Only two things worried her. The first was his name, which she could not pronounce however hard she tried. And the second was her father. If he didn't like walruses, how would he feel about young whatsisname?

But Elspeth need not have worried. As she carried Brrrggch into her father's workroom, an odd look came over his face. And to Elspeth's amazement he started to cry.

Aunt Madge hugged him. Elspeth hugged him. Even Brrrggch hugged him. And Mr. Miller hugged them all back.

"You're an impossible woman, Madge," he said, "but you were right, as always. Your mother loved monsters, Elspeth. She was a really extraordinary person, just like you two. And she would have been so proud of you. I never did know what she saw in me. I'm pretty boring, I'm afraid."

"She saw in you," said Madge with a smile, "someone who was happy to let people be the way they wanted to be. And that is pretty extraordinary, too."

The strange thing was that Elspeth never felt the need to take Brrrggch to school or to tell anyone else about him at all. She didn't even feel the need to wear odd shoes any more. Now that she knew that everyone she loved was extraordinary (and some, like Brrrggch, were even more extraordinary than most), she didn't have to try so hard.

As for Brrrggch, he lived happily ever after. He had found a place where the carpets were never beaten and the slippers were truly smelly. What more could a monster need?

His Majesty
the
Monster

The monarch of Monsterland is a very powerful monster indeed. He has ten winter palaces and twenty-nine summer palaces. His limousines would stretch from one end of the kingdom to the other if they were all on the road at the same time. Of course, that never happens because the the King is the only monster allowed to ride in them. All-powerful as he is, even the King cannot ride in more than one car at a time.

Everyone knows that the King has a huge treasure-house full of jewels and gold bars. It is said that he likes to sit there, in the middle of all his wealth, and put in a few hours of gloating. No one gloats as well as His Majesty, but then no one has so much to gloat about.

The King is not married. It seems that no monsteress in the kingdom was good enough for him. And of course it would be below the dignity of any monster, and especially a king, to marry a non-monster. (In fact, it is hard to imagine any non-monster wishing to marry a monster, but strange things do happen.)

A picture of the King hangs in every town hall in Monsterland. It is a very fine picture, and it shows a very fine monster. He has more heads, and eyes, and legs, and arms, and toes than any monster you have ever met.

A smaller picture of His Majesty, showing only his heads, appears on all the postage stamps of Monsterland. A fine impression of his toes appears on all the coins minted in the kingdom. Banknotes show a complicated picture of the King sitting on his throne. It is complicated because the pose, and the way he has crossed his arms and legs, make it very difficult to tell which way up the picture should be.

One way and another, the citizens of Monsterland see an image of their king almost every day of their lives. If you asked, most of them would probably say that they had seen the King in person, too, on one of his many journeys from one palace to another. Even if they haven't spotted him in one of his limousines, they *feel* as if they have.

The truth, however, is very different. As a matter of fact, *no one* in Monsterland has seen the King. That's right, *no one*. The windows of the royal limousines are black. The windows of the royal palaces have the shutters drawn at all times. The King himself is never seen.

But surely, you may say, the royal servants see the King every day? Again, they would probably say that they do. After all, they very often see the King's robe swishing around the corner. They frequently hear his royal voice bellowing for more soup, or more soap. When a meal has not pleased the King, his servants may even have felt the thwack of a serving dish hitting their heads, thrown by a royal hand. But have they seen the King? Really *seen* him? No. You see, it is the custom in the palace for servants to keep their eyes lowered in the presence of the King. If they dare to look up, they suffer the very worst fate that a monster can suffer. It is so long since this happened that no one can remember quite what the very worst fate is, but the threat obviously works.

How then, you may be asking, was the famous royal portrait, seen in so many town halls, painted? Who designed the royal stamps and bank notes? The answer is a surprising one, but logical. It was the King himself who produced the originals for these works of art. Everyone agrees that Monsterland is lucky to have such a talented ruler—and the talented ruler often reminds them of this.

How? By proclamation, of course. Yes, no one in Monsterland needs to ask what the King does all day. It is perfectly obvious that from morning till night (unless he happens to be painting his own portrait) the King is drafting words of wisdom to be sent out to his subjects. Over a hundred heralds are employed to travel to every part of the kingdom and read in ringing tones the latest proclamations.

Each proclamation begins in the same way:

"I, Aloroso Magneto Kinch-Spoff the Second, Prince of the Five Chimneys, Duke of Ooj, Earl of the Sad Lake and the Onion Hill, Count Murgle and Baron Meddlingwell, do hereby conjure, cajole and chivvy my unworthy subjects..."

After that long beginning, the middle part of the proclamation is usually very short. It might be:

...not to use strawberry-scented soap in their baths, or

...not to dye their hair blue, or

...not to hang their underpants next to their hats when they do their laundry, or

...not to wear green on Tuesdays, or

...not to eat pilchards for breakfast.

After that comes the ending to the proclamation, which is almost as long as the beginning:

"And here be it known, by me, Aloroso Magneto Kinch-Spoff the Second, Prince of the Five Chimneys, Duke of Ooj, Earl of the Sad Lake and the Onion Hill, Count Murgle and Baron Meddlingwell, that any monster ignoring or gnawing this proclamation will be dealt with under the severest penalties of the law, namely, that he shall lose his head (or heads) and work for the rest of his days in the royal salt mines or the royal kitchens, as I, Aloroso Magneto Kinch-Spoff the Second, Prince of the Five Chimneys, Duke of Ooj, Earl of the Sad Lake and the Onion Hill, Count Murgle and Baron Meddlingwell, see fit."

Such proclamations were designed to put fear into the hearts of every monster who read them. Of course, they didn't. For one thing, there were just far too many of them. For another, there weren't any salt mines in Monsterland. Finally, even to monsters, who are not always renowned for their brains, these messages from the King seemed *silly*.

It was, in fact, one of these silly proclamations that started the Great and Glorious Revolution. I will spare you the "I, Aloroso" bit and give you only the message in the middle. Here it is:

"do hereby conjure, cajole and chivvy my unworthy subjects not to put mustard on their pillows."

Now, it would be no trouble to you, I'm sure, if a drop of mustard never again found its way into your bed. Indeed, quite possibly a drop of mustard never *has* found its way into your bed. But monsters are strange creatures (that hardly needs saying), and when they find it hard to sleep, when their babies are crying, when they have toothache or fever of the fangs, they like nothing better than a spoonful or two of freshly made mustard spread on their pillows. It is a monster tradition.

There had been mutterings on street corners about the King's proclamations before, of course. Now, for the first time,

monsters from every part of the kingdom felt that the King had gone too far. Some little inconveniences can be suffered on behalf of one's monarch, but giving up mustard on the pillow is not one of them. Not, at least, if you are a monster.

A conversation that took place in the square at Muncherton is typical of those happening all over the kingdom.

"What I'd like to know," said one large monster, "is why? Why on earth should we give up mustard? Is there a national shortage? Has someone found that it is bad for your fangs or restricts the growth of little monsters? I think not! So I ask again, why?"

"And I," agreed another monster, "ask why have we ever had these wretched proclamations? When have they ever had any point? Are they designed to keep the proclamation-writers busy?"

It was a short step from there for another monster to ask the question that had gradually been building up in the minds of all the monsters present.

"Why," he said, "do we have a King?"

There was a brief silence. Then some of the monsters began to put forward reasons. They were not very good reasons.

"Because we always have!"

"Because this is a kingdom!"

"Because he's there!"

"Because there are a lot of palaces!"

There was silence once more. All the monsters were thinking the same thing. Martelamp Monster took the lead.

"Now, there may be a perfectly good reason behind this proclamation," he said, "but the time has come for us to find out. I suggest that we all visit the King and ask him faces to faces what he has in mind. Who's with me?"

There was the usual confusion that happens when several monsters try to do something together. There was a very long discussion about which palace the King was living in at the moment. There was a very heated argument about the best way to get there. There was a suggestion that they should carry placards and another suggestion that they shouldn't.

At long last, the monsters were on their way.

It wasn't very long before several monsters became hundreds. At every fork in the road, more and more monsters with exactly the same questions on their minds joined the group. When they arrived in front of the palace, over two thousand monsters were already waiting there. The noise and, frankly, the smell was almost overpowering. Gathered together, monsters tend to be a little aggressive. There was a danger that at any moment the natural jostling and nudging of any crowd would break out into a full scale monster-fight. Meanwhile, as well as making a lot of noise, the monsters were trampling the King's flowerbeds in a most disrespectful way.

 Meanwhile, inside the palace, the King was watching from a small window. It was a small window in one of the very smallest rooms in the palace, and the King was having to stand on the you-know-what in order to see out. What he could see worried him very much indeed.

Just then, there came a knock on the door. It was the First Minister, asking His Majesty what should be done.

"Don't interrupt me!" shouted the King angrily. "Can't you see I'm busy worrying?"

"Well, no, Your Majesty," said the First Minister smoothly. "I can't see through the door, you know. But my aim is to stop your worries. I am here," he went on grandly, "to plan our strategy!"

The King had no idea what he was talking about.

"How can you talk about Saturday when I'm in here trying to decide what to do?" he yelled. "What will happen when all those monsters try to get into the palace? We're doomed!"

"No, no, Your Majesty," replied the First Minister soothingly. "My plan is to stop all those monsters from coming in. I suggest that we ask for a delegation only to come into the palace. We can then talk to two or three of the more sensible monsters and find out what they want."

"Delegation? I thought that was what happened to monsterball teams that weren't any good," came the puzzled voice of the King. But he climbed down from the you-know-what because he felt that the First Minister sounded a great deal calmer than he himself felt.

"That's relegation, Your Majesty," said the First Minister. "Don't worry at all. I will set our plan in motion."

The King sighed with relief. It was quite amazing, he thought, how his regal mind always came up with solutions to these little problems. Opening the door just a crack, he made sure that there was no one in the corridor and scuttled back to his private apartments. If he had to talk to monsters, there were preparations he must make.

Outside the palace, the monster crowd was turning ugly. Well, all monster crowds are ugly, but you know what I mean. For one thing, the monsters in this crowd had not eaten since hearing the proclamation some three hours earlier. If there is one thing uglier than an ordinary monster crowd, it is a hungry monster crowd. One or two of the less well-behaved monsters started gnawing at the great iron gates to stave off the foodless feelings in their tummies.

When they saw the First Minister in his robes striding down the steps of the palace, several of the monsters nudged each other and hissed, "The King! The King!" but they were soon hushed. The First Minister didn't have enough heads, for a start.

It was some time before the huge crowd was persuaded to be silent so that the First Minister could be heard. Even when the muttering and mumbling had died down, there was still a good deal of noise from the monsters gnawing the gates. The First Minister summed up the situation

swiftly and ordered buns to be thrown to the crowd. Five thousand buns that had been prepared earlier went hurtling over the gates. Several thousand monsters (for more were coming all the time) suddenly felt much less bothered about the King and his proclamations. At least half of them forgot completely why they had come. The crowd became as silent as it is possible for a crowd to be when several thousand pairs of jaws are munching enthusiastically at monster buns.

"Good monsters of Monsterland," began the First Minister, yelling at the top of his voice, "the King is delighted to see so many of you here today. He would like to invite you all into the palace, but sadly so many monster feet would spoil his new carpets. He asks that three of you be chosen to speak on behalf of all of you."

It is hard to get monsters interested in matters of this kind when their mouths are full of buns. The First Minister assessed the situation in a second, ordered further volleys of buns to be sent across at regular intervals, and grabbed the three monsters nearest the gate to form the delegation. This delegation was reluctant at first, chiefly because it feared that going into the palace would mean no more buns. Reassured on this point, and armed with rations to keep them going for an hour or so, the monsters at last entered the palace behind the First Minister.

Now it so happened that one of the delegation was the Martelamp Monster

we met earlier. He looked around with interest as they were led into the massive throne room. At the very end of the room was a throne of gigantic proportions with someone seated upon it.

"Don't look up!" hissed the First Minster, bowing very low. "Don't you know that you must never look directly at the King? It is very impolite and could be

punished by a very, very long holiday in
His Majesty's salt mines."

The delegation hastily looked at its
feet and bowed like the Minister. Bowing
with more than one head is a rather tricky
business that can confuse even the most
intelligent monster. The delegation took
several minutes to sort itself out.

The King's voice boomed across the
enormous room.

"How can I help you, monsters?
Please speak quickly, as I have a very busy
day ahead of me."

After some shuffling and nudging, Martelamp Monster spoke up.

"Your Majesty," he said, "we have respectfully come to enquire why... that is, what... that is, how... that is, whether..."

"Get on with it!" bellowed the King. "You are making no sense at all. What do you want to know?"

Martelamp was not used to public speaking, especially when the public was a King. He lost his heads completely and blurted out, "We want to know why you make such stupid proclamations!"

There was an awful silence. It was so silent that the sound of several thousand monsters munching several hundred yards away could be heard quite distinctly.

Martelamp trembled. His two companions trembled. The First Minister trembled. They expected the King to be furious … or perhaps icily unpleasant. They didn't expect him to say what he did.

"Well," said the King, and his voice sounded smaller somehow, "what else am I supposed to do?"

Martelamp looked up in surprise. He forgot that he wasn't supposed to look at the King.

"But…" he said.

The second monster looked up, too.

"But…" he said.

The third monster looked up and had a little more to say.

"But," he cried, "*you're* not the King!"

"I am!" cried the King.

Then, in a moment of madness, the First Minister did something he had never done in his twenty years of serving his monster monarch. He, too, looked up.

"But," he stuttered, "y-y-y-y-you don't l-look l-l-l-ike your p-p-p-pictures! N-n-n-not at all!"

"Well, of course not," said the King. "Why do you think I paint them myself? Would you want to look like this?"

Four monsters looked at their King. More monster heads shook sadly. To you or me, the King would have looked fine. To a monster, he looked unimpressive to a high degree. He had one head, two arms and two feet. Worse still, he had two eyes, one nose and one mouth. For a monster, that is quite a lot of heads and arms and

feet and eyes and noses and mouths too few. For a King, a monster King, it is a disaster of huge proportions.

Martelamp had a blinding flash of inspiration.

"Do you mean, Your Majesty," he said, "that during all your reign no one has every actually seen you?"

"Until today," said the King glumly. "And I'm afraid that isn't very good news for *you*."

As a vision of the salt mines loomed again, Martelamp made a quick decision.

"We will never tell another monster," he said, "if you will stop issuing so many proclamations."

"But a good proclamation is the highlight of my day!" cried the King. "How else can I talk to my people?"

There was a pause, then Martelamp spoke. "You could mingle," he said. "You could go out and about, talking to them face to face, or face to faces."

"Mingle?" squeaked the King. "If I mingle, everyone will know I only have ... well, they'll know that my portraits are a little ... *kind*."

"Not," said Martelamp, lowering his voice and playing his masterstroke, "if you mingle anonymously."

The First Minister, who had been standing with his mouths open, grasped at once the brilliance of this plan. He hurried forward and had a few words in the King's even fewer ears.

When Martelamp left the palace a little later and told the crowd that there would be no more silly proclamations, he found several thousand monsters so full of buns they could hardly stand. Most of them needed a small snooze before they could set off for home, but they went quietly enough.

Indeed, there were no proclamations at all for several months. Then, once again, the heralds appeared in town squares.

"I, Aloroso Magneto Kinch-Spoff the Second, Prince of the Five Chimneys, Duke of Ooj, Earl of the Sad Lake and the Onion Hill, Count Murgle and Baron

Meddlingwell, do hereby conjure, cajole and chivvy my unworthy subjects…" he began, "to use strawberry-scented soap in their baths, to dye their hair blue, to hang their underpants next to their hats when they do their laundry, to wear green on Tuesdays, to eat pilchards for breakfast and, most importantly, to spread mustard on their pillows *whenever they want to*. And here be it known, by me, Aloroso Magneto Kinch-Spoff the Second, Prince of the Five Chimneys, Duke of Ooj, Earl of the Sad Lake and the Onion Hill, Count Murgle and Baron Meddlingwell, that any monster ignoring or, indeed, gnawing this proclamation will be dealt with under the severest penalties of the law, namely, that he shall lose his head (or heads) and work for the rest of his days in the royal salt mines or the royal kitchens, as I, Aloroso etc. etc."

There was a mighty cheer from every monster in Monsterland.

"Long live the King!" cried an old monster in green.

"Long live the King!" yelled a middle-aged monster in delight.

"Ong ive uh Kin!" howled a very young monster in nappies.

"Thanks very much," said a small and insignificant monster in dark glasses. "Ooops! I mean, long live the King!"

Monster
Prints

Darren wanted to do everything his brother did. But Mark was seven years older than his little brother and often wasn't at all interested in the things a six-year-old likes.

One summer, Darren became very interested in monsters. He read books about them. He drew pictures of them. He watched videos and made up stories about them. Finally, he announced that he was going on a monster hunt and would not be coming back until he had *found* a monster.

"Oh, right," said Mark, reading a book as he munched his breakfast cereal. Mark also had an interest this summer, but it was archaeology. He had found a small fossil on the nearby hillside and was very keen to find some more.

"I mean it," said Darren. "I'm going to take something to eat and my monster-hunting tools, and I'm not coming back without one. If you don't believe me, just wait and see."

"Mmmmm, okay," said Mark, who was somewhere back in the Jurassic Period and hadn't listened to a word.

Mark spent the day hunting for fossils. He had a small hammer, which he used for breaking open likely-looking stones. He found a coin, an empty sweet wrapper and a small lizard, but no fossils.

Darren spent the day hunting for monsters. He had a feeling that they liked dark, damp places, so he crawled about in the wild bit of woodland at the bottom of the garden. He found a snail, three worms, some broken eggshells and a mouldy apple core, but no monsters.

That evening, Mark's mother asked him where Darren was.

"Mark, put that book away when I'm talking to you," she said, "have you seen your little brother?"

"No," said Mark, still thinking about dinosaurs.

"Well, do you know what he was going to be doing today?"

"No, oh, he said something about not coming back," said Mark.

"Mark! What are you talking about? Just concentrate, please! What do you mean he isn't coming back? Where has he gone?"

"I don't know," said Mark, and for the first time he felt a little uneasy. What was it that Darren had said that morning?

"Well, was he upset about something? Had you done something to worry him? Has he run away?"

Mark couldn't help, and his mother rushed upstairs to check what Darren had taken. She was relieved to find that his clothes were still in the cupboard. She was even more relieved to find that his favourite

monster books were still on the shelf. She knew that he wouldn't go anywhere at all without those. But he hadn't come back for his supper, and it would soon be dark.

Mark and his mother went out into the garden and started calling. Their voices sounded more and more desperate as they yelled the little boy's name over and over again. Their next-door neighbour, hearing the noise, came out to see if he could help. His voice soon joined the others when he heard the story.

It was very gloomy when the three searchers reached the woods that linked the properties. There were brambles that caught at their clothes and tree roots to fall over.

"Darren! Darren!" they called.

Just when it seemed that they would never find him, there came a scrabbling sound in the undergrowth.

"I'm here!" called a little voice, "but I can't come out."

"Thank goodness! Why not?" asked his mother, crouching down in front of a group of bushes.

"I can't come home until I've found a monster," said Darren. "That's what I said, and you told me I must always do something if I've said I will."

"Even monster-hunters have to eat and sleep, Darren," said his mother. "It's not a case of not doing what you said, it's a case of retreating to fight another day."

"Oh, good, but I still can't come out," said Darren after a pause.

"Why not?"

"I've got stuck on some brambles."

"Well, just pull them off. Are you hurt?" asked his mother.

"No, but my shorts are," replied the intrepid monster-hunter. "They've got a big hole in them and it's embarrassing."

"Darren, don't be ridiculous! It's only me and Mark here!" Darren's mother waved goodbye to the neighbour and mouthed "Thanks very much!" in the gathering darkness.

A rather subdued monster-hunter came out of the bushes, trying to hide the back of his shorts with his hands. Mark and his mother did their best not to laugh as the monster-hunter ordered them to walk in front of him and scuttled up the stairs as soon as he got inside.

Next morning at breakfast, the boys' mother spoke seriously.

"I must know roughly where you are," she said, "so today I think it would be best if you, Mark, took Darren with you. Don't let him fall down any cliffs or get trapped in caves. You are much older, so I'm holding you responsible."

"Oh, Mum!" cried Mark. "I can't find any fossils with him hanging around!"

"Oh, Mum!" cried Darren. "I can't find any monsters with him there!"

"I don't see why not," said their mother. "There's absolutely no reason why there shouldn't be just as many monsters on a hillside as in a wood. And I can't see why it should affect your fossil-hunting at all, Mark. I've made up my mind, so just get on with it. I'll make you both some sandwiches."

The fossil-hunter and the monster-hunter trooped off eventually, neither looking too happy. When they reached the hillside, Mark made it clear that he wanted to be left in peace. He picked up his special hammer and started thwacking a piece of rock as hard as he could.

"Stop! Stop! Stop!" shouted Darren. "You'll frighten them all away! I'll never find a monster if you keep doing that."

"And I'll never find a fossil if I don't," said Mark. "You'll just have to put up with it. Sit quietly over there and find me some nice round rocks like this one. You can be a fossil-finder's assistant for

today, and tomorrow, if I have time, I'll help you look for monsters."

Darren didn't feel he had much choice, but it was boring looking at stones. He started asking Mark about fossils and was surprised to find it was interesting. Mark was surprised, too. Explaining about something you are very keen on is fun, and Darren asked some quite sensible questions.

"The fossil you found was of a leaf, wasn't it?" he queried. "Is that the only kind of fossil you can find around here?"

"No," said Mark, "but it's the only kind of fossil I'm likely to find. A chap on the other side of this hill found—you'll like this—some fossilized poo."

"Fossilized poo! I don't believe it! You're making it up!" laughed Darren.

"Nope, it was fossilized dinosaur poo. It was in all the papers."

"I don't want you to find any," said Darren firmly. "I'll never hear the last of it if my brother is in the paper with poo."

"I wouldn't be that lucky," replied Mark. And he sounded so sad about it that Darren started sorting out stones a bit more carefully. It would be nice, after all, if one of them could find something good today.

As they worked, Mark told Darren about his dreams of becoming a proper palaeontologist. It was the longest and best conversation the boys had had for some time. Darren found himself admiring his brother even more. Mark found that Darren was a good listener.

"If you find a new dinosaur," he told his little brother, "you can sometimes decide what to name it. I might find the very first Markosaurus."

Darren thought that sounded good and worked even harder, but after a while he got fed up with sorting rocks. It was time to eat their sandwiches, so he wandered around munching at his and kicking at the ground. The hillside was very bare, with big slabs of rock lying out in the sun. Darren kicked harder at a huge stone—just for something to do. To his horror, it began to slide, skidding down the slope towards Mark, who had his back turned.

"Look out!" screamed Darren. Mark turned, saw what was happening and threw himself to one side just in time. The stone, and Mark's hammer, went skittering on down the slope, stopping with a crash near some big boulders.

"I'm so sorry! I'm so sorry!" Darren was almost in tears as he ran to hug his brother. "Are you all right?"

Mark was white-faced, but he was relieved that Darren hadn't slipped with the stone. He had promised to take care of him, after all.

"What exactly did you do?" he asked. "Show me!"

Darren walked carefully to where the stone had become dislodged. Hidden no longer, a flat slab of rock gleamed in the sun—and so did a perfect set of footprints!

"Mark!" he yelled, "there has been a monster here!"

"It's not a monster," said Mark, falling to his knees. "It's a dinosaur's prints. And I've never seen anything like it! Darren, you found a fossil! It's brilliant!"

"I'm going to count it as a monster," said Darren, "because that's what I was looking for, but you can count it as a dinosaur if you like. What do we do now?"

"We have to go and tell someone before someone else finds it!" cried Mark, his eyes shining. "Come on!"

As they trotted down the hill, Darren started to laugh.

"If it's a new dinosaur," he said, "it might be a Markosaurus after all."

"It might just be a Darrenosaurus," grinned his brother. "You never know!"